D0189945

Flint

by

Chris Powling

Illustrated by Alan Marks

700032474508

WORCESTERSHIRE COUNTY COUNCIL	
450	
Bertrams	07.06.08
	£5.99
EV	

First published in 2008 in Great Britain by
Barrington Stoke Ltd
18 Walker St, Edinburgh, EH3 7LP

www.barringtonstoke.co.uk

Copyright © 2008 Chris Powling
Illustrations © Alan Marks

The moral right of the author has been asserted in
accordance with the Copyright, Designs and
Patents Act 1988

ISBN: 978-1-84299-532-7

Printed in Great Britain by Bell & Bain Ltd

A Note from the Author

I've always found pirates exciting – to read about, that is. In real life they must have been hard and cruel. So maybe you had to be just as hard, and just as cruel, to get the better of them. That's what this story is about.

For
Cap'n Jake, Cap'n Polly
and Cap'n Suzie,
my favourite pretend-pirates

Contents

Chapter 1

Prisoners

It's the stink that gets to me.

Can it be rats?

Maybe it's the foul water all round us.
The crew call it *bilge* water. One sniff makes
me want to throw up.

I can put up with the darkness. I can put up with the clink of chains when I move. What I can't stand is the smell down here on the bottom deck.

The old officer – they call him the *bosun* – taps my arm. "Open your mouth, Edmund," he says. "And hold your nose. That may help."

"Will it?"

"Try."

And it does help ... for a bit. But soon the vile smell is back as strong as ever. It's like a fog hanging in the air.

"When will they set us free, bosun?" I ask.

He gives a snort – a dry, old-man's snort. "These are pirates, son. You can never tell with pirates. Sometimes they treat you like a prince. Sometimes worse than a dog. It all depends on their mood. Also on what they want from us."

"Such as?"

"Help with the ship, maybe. A bit of sail-making, perhaps. Or working one of the guns ..."

"So we become pirates too, you mean?"

"For a while, yes. Pirates are a tricky lot, Edmund. You've got to be as tricky as they are if you want to stay alive. We may not have to be pirates for long – just till we get a change of luck."

"I'd rather die, thank you."

The old man sucks on a tooth. "You're lucky, then. You'll probably get your wish on this man's ship."

"Flint," I said.

"Cap'n Flint to us. Slit your throat soon as look at you, Flint would. Then wipe his dagger across your shirt by way of a send-off. That's what I've heard, anyways."

****

I've heard the stories myself. Even someone new to the sea like me knows all

---

about Captain Flint. Most ships flee in terror

when they see his flag. That's if they don't

surrender at once without a shot being fired.

Flint doesn't care which it is. "I loves a good

chase," he always says. "And I loves an easy

kill, too."

Either way, it will be blood-and-guts

before nightfall.

Our blood.

And our guts.

So why aren't we dead already, the old bosun and me? Where is Flint taking us? There's something in the wind all right. No wonder I feel as sick as a pig down here in the ship's hold – as if the Devil himself has just farted in my face.

Chapter 2

Cat O' Nine Tails

An hour later they come for us. There are four of them. They slide our chains loose from the planking. They unlock the shackles from our hands and feet. Then they bundle us up to the main deck. That's where the rest of the crew are waiting.

Also Captain Flint himself.

He's as tall and thin as a boat-hook. He's as sharp as a cut-throat razor. He's as smooth as silk round your neck. Now look at his elegant clothes – from his black three-cornered hat down to his shoes with silver buckles. Finish off with a cutlass, a dagger and a pair of gleaming pistols.

That's Flint.

Even his voice makes my heart miss a beat. It's as cold as a stab in the back. "Ah," he says. "Our guests ..."

"I'm no guest of yours," I snap. "You and your men dragged me aboard at gunpoint."

"Did we?" says Flint and he smiles as sweet as a shark. "Now why would we need a snooty young gent like you?" he asks. "And a gritty old salt like the bosun? We've got plenty of crew already."

This is true. I've never seen so many pirates crammed in so small a space. Some pirates slouch along the ship's rail. Some slump on cannons and coils of rope. Some peer down from the masts and rigging. All of them are armed to the teeth. And all of them have the lean and hungry look of an animal that's tasted blood. It takes me a moment to spot where the blood is coming from.

He's roped to the ship's wheel. His bare, criss-crossed back is shredded to the bone.

He was our captain when the pirates captured the ship three days ago.

Flint turns his nose up in disgust. "Just look at him," he scoffs. "Soft as a girl. 76 lashes was all he could take. I ask you, where's the sport in that?"

"What about these two, Cap'n?" someone calls.

"Them?" says Flint, coolly.

His eyes slide over the bosun and me. "Now there's a pretty idea," he says. "What do you say, my lads? Shall we feed 'em both to the cat – lick by lovely lick?"

"The cat?" I whisper.

"The whip, Edmund," the old bosun groans. "See it dangling down his back? It's called the cat o' nine tails."

The bosun's eyes are rolling in his head. He's swaying on his feet. It's clear he's had enough. There's a loud cheer from the pirates as he falls in a dead faint.

16

Chapter 3

A Trip Ashore

But it's only a joke. About the cat o' nine tails, I mean. Flint has other plans for us on this grey, muggy morning.

Soon, we're in a rowing boat. The bosun is still out cold. I'm doing my best to row. Flint sits facing the boat's prow. He holds a

loaded pistol. He's not taking any chances –
not even with a bit-of-boy like me and a worn
-out wreck like the bosun. "Keep her steady,"
Flint growls.

"Where are we going, Captain?" I ask.

"Ashore, my dear."

He jabs a finger ahead of us. It's land all
right. The mist on the water had been hiding
it till now. But this is no island paradise. It's
more like a floating jungle. I can feel the
heat, the flies and the sickly fever. A shiver

runs down my spine. "Is that your plan?"
I choke. "You're going to leave us here?"

"Maroon you?" Flint almost smiles. "You
think the two of you are worth marooning,
my dear? A useless old jack tar? And a
spoilt young gent who fancied a sea-trip just
for the fun of it? Why should I waste a good
marooning on the likes of you?"

"So what will we do ashore, Captain?"
I say.

"We'll bury this," Flint tells me.

He stretches out a leg. With the toe of a silver-buckled shoe, he lifts the canvas that lies between us. Under it is the biggest sea-chest I've ever seen. "Open the lid," Flint says. "Take a peep inside."

It's stuffed with treasure.

I see gold and silver, I see rings and jewels, I see spoons and dishes and goblets – also a dagger, a set of pistols, and a sword fit for an admiral. And that's just on top. I can only wonder at the riches I can't see.

Slowly, I shut the lid of the sea-chest. I pick up the oars again. "Do the crew know about this?" I ask.

"About hiding the treasure?" says Flint. "They voted for it, my dear. Right now, every spy-glass on the ship is watching us. It's always share and share alike with pirates."

He leans forward over the sea-chest. "Well, almost always," he says. "In this case, they know what we're hiding. What they don't know is where we're hiding it. That's my little secret. Soon it will be your little secret as well."

He smiles his evil, shark-like smile.

Our little secret as well? I think to myself.

That's when I see the old bosun has woken up. His eyes are wide with terror as he stares at Flint. And I can see why. Now we know he means to kill us.

Chapter 4

X Marks the Spot

Don't ask how far we lug the sea-chest.
The island is bigger than it looks. We
stagger over boggy ground through thick
jungle and tangled creepers. The bosun and
I do all the carrying. Flint covers up any
tracks we make.

Every so often we catch a sight of the sea. The old man gives a sob of despair every time. He stumbles and falls. I yank him back on his feet as fast as I can.

By noon we're both worn out.

Our faces are grey with fear. Every bit of us is painful. Even Flint himself seems weary. His frilly shirt hangs loose. His shoes are clogged with mud. Only his eyes have kept their glitter. Just like his weapons.

He's pointing a pistol at us now. "This place will do very well," he nods.

"Here?" says the bosun.

"Right here."

I can see why he's picked it. It's easy to miss a clearing as small as this. It's creepy, too – what with the mass of thorns all round us. Flint scuffs a cross in the dirt with the heel of his shoe. "X marks the spot," he says. "That's where you dig."

"With our bare hands?" I ask.

"With your bare teeth if you prefer," spits Flint. "Make the hole deep enough for the sea-chest. Also long enough ..."

"Yes?"

"... for the two of *you*."

We hear a sudden flapping of wings. A pair of vultures have landed on a tree close by. Vultures, yes. Vile creatures who feed on corpses. People call them the Birds of Death.

31

Chapter 5

Digging Our Own Graves

The digging itself is sheer agony. Soon our finger-nails are split and our hands are torn to shreds. Sweat runs into our eyes. The bosun taps his heart. "It's my ticker," he groans. "I can't go on much longer ..."

"Keep digging," says Flint.

"Captain, he's about to keel over!" I say.

"So?"

Flint sits propped on the trunk of a fallen tree. His eyes dart this way and that. He fingers the trigger of his pistol. We jump at every move he makes. We know the vultures are watching us, too. Sooner or later they'll have rich pickings.

Little by little, the pit gets deeper.

By mid-afternoon, the bosun and I can heave the sea chest into it. There's room for two bodies as well. We hear the clink of Flint's cutlass as he rises to his feet. "Finished?" he hisses.

"No ... no ..." wheezes the old man.

"Bosun!" I yelp.

He can hardly breathe. It's as if his heart has stopped in mid-beat. His mouth sags open in a horrible last-gasp grin.

He falls beside the sea chest.

I watch in horror as he kicks and twists in pain. Slowly, the frenzy fades. At last, he's lying still. He's just a bundle of rags and dirt now. For the bosun it's all over.

But it isn't over for me.

Chapter 6

An Easy Kill

Flint crosses the clearing. He lifts his pistol. He has no reason to keep me alive now and every reason to kill me. The vultures are still perched on the tree behind him. They've never looked so evil and ugly. If they had any lips they'd be licking them.

I haven't got a hope in Hell.

Maybe that's why I'm not scared any more. I just don't care. Also I'm caked with dirt from top to toe. Just about every part of my body has a cut, a scrape or a bruise.

Yet somehow my fear has vanished.

Maybe Flint can see this. He narrows his eyes till each is no more than a slit in his hard, cruel face. "Are you ready to die?" he asks. "Like your doddery old friend?"

"Ready when you are," I say.

He hears the scorn in my voice and takes a step towards me. I smile and take a step towards him. "There," I say. "Now we're really close. You can't miss."

"Are you mocking me, my dear?"

"Mocking you? The famous Captain Flint? I wouldn't dare! I've heard you like an easy kill, that's all. Oh, is that the problem? That I'm still on my feet?"

And I stroll past him to the fallen tree trunk. I sit myself down. "Go ahead, Captain," I say. "I promise I won't fight back."

Flint turns round to face me.

But he still keeps his temper. He tucks the pistol back in his belt. He slides his cutlass out of its sheath. He swishes it from side to side till it zings in the air like sharp, steely music. He's about to slice off my head. "One swipe should do it," he says.

He lines up the cutlass.

That's when I can't help shutting my eyes.

Chapter 7

The Final Blow

What does a cutlass sound like as it slices into its target ... a target of skin and bone, I mean?

That's what I hear next.

But it isn't *my* skin and bone.

My eyes blink open, amazed. Flint is struggling to stay on his feet. Blood is running down his chin. As I stare at him, he sinks to his knees. Then he falls flat on his face in front of me. There's a sword in his back. It's a trim, elegant sword. It's a sword fit for an admiral.

Or maybe fit for a bosun.

The old man looms over Flint. He puts his foot on Flint's back. He pulls out the sword and wipes it clean across Flint's shirt. "By way of a send-off," he says.

"But you were dead!" I gasp.

"That's what I wanted you to think.
I wanted this scum of a pirate to think so,
too. It's why I've been weeping and wailing
and making a damn fool of myself. If you
want to stay alive with pirates you've got to
be as tricky as they are ..."

"But what about Flint's crew?" I ask.

"In chains already, I fancy," the bosun
says. "The Royal Navy has arrived. Didn't

you see the man o' war coming round the head-land?"

"No," I say.

"Neither did Flint. His mind was on his treasure. Speaking of which, we must bury it fast."

"Bury the treasure?" I ask.

"You want the Navy to grab the lot, Edmund? They can have Flint's body. That'll pay for our passage home. Later, when the coast is clear, we'll hire a ship. We'll come back here to fetch our fortune, you and me. I reckons we deserve every penny!"

The bosun looks younger and richer already. His grin is somehow ... *Flinty*. Even the vultures have flapped away into the jungle. It's as if they know he's the man in charge now. Besides, he's saved my life as well as his own.

Who am I to argue with that?

Barrington Stoke would like to thank all its readers for commenting on the manuscript before publication and in particular:

Ali Basharat

Gemma Harrison

Diane Hayes

Susan Kaye

Reece M.

Emma Milner

Sarah Moxon

Josh R.

Become a Consultant!

Would you like to give us feedback on our titles before they are published? Contact us at the email address below – we'd love to hear from you!

info@barringtonstoke.co.uk
www.barringtonstoke.co.uk

Great reads – no problem!

Barrington Stoke books are:

Great stories – from thrillers to comedy to horror, and all by the best writers around!

No hassle – fast reads with no boring bits, and a story that doesn't let go of you till the last page.

Short – the perfect size for a fast, fun read.

We use our own font and paper to make it easier to read our books. And we ask teenagers like you, who want a no-hassle read, to check every book before it's published.

That way, we know for sure that every Barrington Stoke book is a great read for everyone.

Check out www.barringtonstoke.co.uk for more info about Barrington Stoke and our books!

If you loved this book
why don't you read ...

Fight
by Chris Powling

**Matt's mate is a big, tough guy.
So that must make Matt hard too ...
Or does it?**

gr8reads

You can order *Fight* directly from our website at
www.barringtonstoke.co.uk

If you loved this book

why don't you read ...

Gremlin

by Chris Powling

The pilot is sick.
The plane will crash.
Can Glenn save it?

gr8reads

You can order *Gremlin* directly from our website at
www.barringtonstoke.co.uk

If you loved this book

why don't you read ...

Blade

by Chris Powling

They tell Rich to stay away from Toxon.
They tell him about the blade too, and what it
can do to you.
But Rich is in the wrong place at the
wrong time.

gr8reads

You can order *Blade* directly from our website at
www.barringtonstoke.co.uk

If you loved this book

why don't you read ...

Thing

by Chris Powling

Black button eyes.
Zig-zag mouth.
Stiff body.
Thing.

Once it was Robbie's best friend.

Now it's become his enemy ...

**You can order *Thing* directly from our website at
www.barringtonstoke.co.uk**